The Lady
IN THE
Blue Cloak

The Lady
IN THE
Blue Cloak

Legends from the Texas Missions

retold by

ERIC A. KIMMEL

illustrated by

SUSAN GUEVARA

Holiday House / NEW YORK

To Anna Cruz, Gloria Montalvo,
and the children of San Benito, Texas
E. A. K.

For Miguel Lopez
S. G.

Thanks are due to Elizabeth Dupree of the San Antonio Missions for all her help,
as well as to Eida del Risco of Lectorum Publications, Inc., for her help with the Spanish language.

Text copyright © 2006 by Eric A. Kimmel
Illustrations copyright © 2006 by Susan Guevara
All Rights Reserved
Printed in the United States of America
The text typeface is Galliard.
The artwork was created with oil paint on canvas.
www.holidayhouse.com
First Edition
1 3 5 7 9 10 8 6 4 2

Library of Congress Cataloging-in-Publication Data
Kimmel, Eric A.
The lady in the blue cloak : legends from the Texas missions /
retold by Eric A. Kimmel ; illustrated by Susan Guevara.—1st ed.
p. cm.
Includes bibliographical references (p. 32).
Summary: A collection of stories depicting the history of four Texas missions
from the 17th century to the 19th century.
ISBN 0-8234-1738-7 (hardcover)
1. Children's stories, American. [1. Missions—Texas—Fiction.
2. Indians of North America—Texas—Fiction.
3. Texas—History—To 1846—Fiction.
4. Short stories.] I. Guevara, Susan, ill. II. Title.
PZ7.K5648Lad 2006
[Fic]—dc22
2004054167
ISBN-13: 978-0-8234-1738-4
ISBN-10: 0-8234-1738-7

Contents

Introduction

The first Spanish friars to come to Texas could not have encountered a more challenging environment if they had landed on the moon. The horse tribes of the plains, the Kiowas and Comanches, preferring to retain their way of life, wanted no part of Spanish law, government, or religion. The missions were built as forts as well as churches, because they were constantly threatened with attack.

Adapting to a new culture and new traditions was extremely difficult for the hunting and gathering tribes who chose to cluster around the missions for food and protection. Becoming farmers and Christians required a total break with their past. The padres are often condemned as agents of imperialism. There is some truth in this. However, it must be remembered that they sincerely believed they were doing God's work, saving lives as well as souls.

This violent conflict among the indigenous and European cultures, which continued for many years, ultimately led to the growth of a new culture—one that combined elements of both European and American civilazations.

The Lady in the Blue Cloak
(Misión de San Francisco de los Tejas)

Father Damián Manzanet and his fellow padres arrived in Texas in 1689. They came upon a village of Tejas Indians. The Tejas people greeted them with great joy, as if they were expecting them. Their chief told the padres, "You are our honored guests. We are happy to see you. Our friend promised you would come. We have waited a long time for you."

Father Damián was puzzled. What did the chief mean? As far as he knew, his was the first mission to enter the Tejas country. How could the Tejas know anything about them? Who was the friend who told of their coming?

Father Damián asked the chief these questions. The chief answered by telling him a strange story.

"Our friend is a beautiful lady who often comes to visit our people. She is kind and gentle. She helps those who are sick and comforts those who are sad. We asked where she came from. She told us her home is a land far away, on the other side of the wide ocean. A spirit called God sent her to us. We asked her to tell us more about God. The lady said that God made all the creatures who live in the sky or on the earth. God rules over the heavens. When people die, they go above the clouds to live with God. All people are God's children. God loves them and cares about them. God never forgets about them, no matter how far away they might be.

"We had many questions about God. More than our friend could answer. She promised that one day men from a distant land would come to us. We would recognize them by their brown and gray robes and the sandals they wore on their feet. These men would be our teachers. She told us to welcome them as friends. They would answer our questions. They would help us to come closer to God. Now you are here, and it is exactly as our friend promised."

The chief pointed to a soldier wearing a blue cloak. "I want some cloth like that—the color of the sky. I will give you shells and rabbit skins in exchange. But it must be that color."

"You may have the cloth as a gift. Only tell me why it must be blue," Father Damián asked.

The chief explained. "Our friend, the beautiful lady, always wears a cloak of that color when she comes to visit us. My grandmother has died. I want to bury her in such a cloth. I want her to have a beautiful cloak to wear when the lady takes her to meet God."

"You will have a blue cloak," Father Damián promised. "I will give you all the blue cloth that we have. Then I will answer all your questions about God."

Father Damián and his fellow padres lived with the Tejas people for many months, answering their questions and teaching them about God. The Tejas people taught the padres as well. They learned many things about the new country and the people who lived there. They also shared many stories about their special friend, the Lady in the Blue Cloak.

"We are so happy you have come," they told the padres. "Everything the lady told us about you is true."

Yet try as they might, Father Damián and his fellow padres could never learn more about the mysterious lady. Was she a ghost? A spirit? Or perhaps an angel, sent down by God himself from heaven.

Father Damián went back south, to what is now Mexico, at the end of the year. He returned the following year, bringing tools, farm animals, and seeds, and experts to teach the Tejas how to use them.

The Tejas people came from the surrounding countryside to greet the returning padres. "We knew you had come back. The Lady in the Blue Cloak came to visit us. She told us you had returned to build a house for God. We want to help you. We want God to live among us. The Lady also promised you would bring us new plants, new animals. Everything she said has come true. We will never be hungry and cold. We will never be afraid of our enemies. God is our friend. God and the Lady in the Blue Cloak will protect us."

And with the help of the Tejas, the padres began building a mission six miles west of the Neches River. They called it San Francisco de los Tejas.

Not one of the padres could explain the story of the Lady in the Blue Cloak. Yet the Tejas people never doubted her existence. They were not making up a fairy tale. They had seen this person. They had spoken with her. They knew she was real. But who was she?

Years later, one of the padres who had accompanied Father Damián returned to Spain. He learned of a holy nun, Sister María Coronel, who lived in the town of Agreda. Sister María was known to have visions. While in a trance, she would visit a distant land far away in the New World. There she met people whose clothes and customs were very different from those of Spain. She became friends with these people and told them about God. And they listened. But they still had many questions, more than Sister María could answer. She promised that God would send proper teachers to them one day. In the meantime, they were not to fear, because God loved them.

The padre traveled to Agreda to meet Sister María. To his sorrow, he learned that she had died many years before. However, she had written about her visions in a journal and letters. The padre read her descriptions of the faraway people she met in her visions. "These are the Tejas people! How could Sister María describe them so perfectly? When did she visit the New World?"

"Sister María never visited the New World," the other nuns told him. "She was born in Agreda and died here."

The padre visited Sister María's grave. He said prayers for her soul in the chapel. Before leaving, the nuns asked if he might wish to see some objects that had belonged to Sister María. They showed the padre her prayer book, her rosary, and a woolen cloak that she always wore whenever she went outside.

It was a beautiful blue.

Rosa's Window
(Misión de San José y San Miguel de Aguayo)

At one time the Mission of San José and San Miguel de Aguayo was one of the most beautiful in all the Spanish colonies. For many years it stood in ruins, but now it has been restored so a visitor can imagine what it looked like in its days of glory. The carvings around the main entrance, the windows, and the inner chapel are treasures of Spanish mission art.

These carvings are said to be the work of one man, a famous carpenter named Pedro Huizar. The padres invited him to come all the way from Spain to carve decorations for their newly built mission church. Pedro was reluctant to go. He was engaged to be married to a young woman named Rosa, whom he loved deeply. He did not want to leave her. Who knew what perils he might encounter crossing the sea? Who knew what dangers might befall him in the distant land of Texas, at the farthest borders of New Spain? Pedro feared that if he left Rosa behind, he might never see her again.

Rosa persuaded him to go. The mission padres were poor, but the order of the Franciscan Friars, which sent out the padres and supervised the missions, was extremely wealthy. Pedro had been offered a handsome fee, more than enough to allow a young couple to afford a fine house and servants. The couple would only be apart for a few years. More important, Pedro would be doing God's work. To worship in a beautiful church decorated with exquisite carvings would give the faraway people of Texas a taste of heaven. The beauty created by Pedro's hands would bring these new Christians closer to God.

Pedro agreed to go, both for his love of God and for his love of Rosa. After many months, he arrived at the Mission of San José and San Miguel de Aguayo. He set to work. The native people watched him carving the stone. The padres asked him to teach some of the younger boys who wished to become stone carvers, too. Pedro learned their language. He in turn taught them to speak Spanish. The boys would be able to carry on the work of building and decorating churches when Pedro returned to Spain.

Pedro Huizar remained at the mission for two years. One day a letter arrived from Spain. It brought sad news. Rosa had died. Pedro's fears had come true. The one he hoped to make his bride was gone. He would never see her again.

Pedro cast his tools aside. He could not work; he could not eat. He took to his bed. His life seemed worthless. He only wanted to die.

The padres came to comfort Pedro. They told him not to grieve for Rosa, who was surely with God in heaven. Instead of wishing to die, he must use the talents that God had given him to create something in Rosa's memory.

The padres had shown Pedro the way. He must create something special in honor of God, and in honor of Rosa. He got up from his bed for the first time in weeks. He walked around the church. At the south side, by the big baptistery window, he stopped. Here he would carve his masterpiece.

Pedro Huizar worked at that window for the next five years. Carving it brought him peace. He told the padres that God guided his hands.

The graceful forms that Pedro carved around that window have made it one of the gems of American art. It is still called *Rosa's Window* in memory of the young woman who died long ago across the sea.

Some say that if you walk by the mission on a clear night, when the ruined walls cast long shadows through the mesquite, you can hear the murmuring voices of the padres in prayer. And if you look closely, you might see two figures framed by the sacristy window, a man and a woman, dressed in the clothes of Old Spain.

The Bell

(Misión de San José y San Miguel de Aguayo)

Soon after the Mission of San José and San Miguel de Aguayo was established, a group of padres came out from Spain to help with the work of teaching and preaching to the native people. One of the padres asked his cousin, Don Ángel de Léon, an officer in the Spanish army, to come along.

"I am a soldier, not a priest!" Don Ángel protested.

"All the more reason for you to join us," his cousin insisted. "You have faithfully served the king for many years. Now it is time for you to serve God."

"But I am going to be married!"

"We will let your bride, Doña Teresa, decide."

Doña Teresa, a young woman from a noble family, did not hesitate. She told Don Ángel, "As much as I love you, I cannot keep you for myself. There is important work for you in the New World, serving both God and our king. I cannot ask you to stay with me when I know how much the padres need you."

"I will only be gone one year," Don Ángel told her. "We will be married when I return."

Before he left for the New World, Don Ángel gave his future bride a ring and a cross on a chain, all made of the finest gold. He told Doña

Teresa, "I give you this cross and this ring as a promise of my return. I pledge my devotion to you, even unto death."

Doña Teresa placed the ring on her finger and the cross around her neck. "And I promise you that I will be faithful to you. I will never take this ring from my finger or this chain from around my neck until you come back to me."

They embraced. Then Don Ángel and the padres boarded their ship. Doña Teresa stood on the shore, watching until its masts disappeared below the horizon.

The ship landed at the port of Veracruz in New Spain, and those on board began the long journey north to Texas. Don Ángel commanded the soldiers who would accompany the padres. Most of the men who served in the ranks were criminals and convicts. They needed a strong officer such as Don Ángel to keep them in line.

By the time the padres reached the Texas mission, Don Ángel had turned his collection of convicts into real soldiers. He loved this exciting new country. In his letters to Doña Teresa he described its birds, animals, and flowers. He wrote of the adventures he had every day.

"After we are married I will bring you here," he wrote. "I want to show you the New World. It is my hope that we can begin our life together here."

Doña Teresa's reply took many months to cross the ocean. "My deepest hope is to be wherever you are. My life will be with you."

These words would have brought Don Ángel great joy. Sadly, he never read them. By the time the letter arrived, he was dead.

It happened this way. A band of Lipan Apache raiders attacked without warning. Two workers and one of the padres were killed in the fields. Others raced for the shelter of the mission. The soldiers, led by Don Ángel, charged out to meet the attackers. They drove them off after a fierce fight.

As the Apaches galloped away, one turned and shot an arrow. It struck Don Ángel in the neck. He fell from his horse, badly wounded.

The soldiers carried their commander back to the mission. The padres saw that Don Ángel was dying. With his last words he spoke of his love for Doña Teresa. "Tell her not to mourn for me. I free her from her vows," he whispered. "It is my hope that she will find happiness with someone else, someone who will love her as much as I have."

The padres buried Don Ángel in the mission churchyard. They wrote a letter to Doña Teresa in Spain, telling her the tragic news.

Doña Teresa read the letter. She did not weep. Instead, she took to her bed. She lay there for days, staring at the ceiling, never speaking a word. Her frightened family sent for the parish priest. He pleaded with her to get up, to take some nourishment. Don Ángel's death was a tragedy, he said, but it was also God's will. She must accept it and continue to live. To do less would be to deny God's goodness and wisdom.

Doña Teresa turned her face to the wall. Her family did not know what to do next. They feared she would die of grief.

Now it happened that the same ship that brought the padres' letter to Doña Teresa brought another letter from the padres to a foundry in a nearby town. It was an order for a bell for the recently completed bell tower of the Mission of San José and San Miguel de Aguayo. Once the bell was in place, the work of building the church would be complete.

Doña Teresa's sister told her that this bell was being cast. Doña Teresa's eyes opened. She sat up in bed. She put her feet on the floor and stood up for the first time in weeks. "Help me get dressed," she said to her sister. "I must see the bell."

Doña Teresa's family rode with her in a coach to the foundry. A large crowd had gathered, waiting for the exciting moment when the molten bronze would be poured into the mold. The foundry master gave Doña Teresa the place of honor. "I know this bell has special meaning for you," he said.

Doña Teresa replied, "This bell will always be precious to me." As the metal began to flow, she took the ring from her finger and the gold cross and chain from around her neck and dropped them into the mold. She spoke to the bell:

"My beloved Don Ángel gave this ring and cross to me when he sailed for the New World. They are all I have of the one I love. I wish with all my heart that I could sail across the ocean with you to weep beside his grave. Alas, I cannot. I give you these precious gifts. I know Don Ángel will hear your sweet peals when you ring the Angelus over his grave. Tell him that I was faithful to him. I waited for him, and I loved him to the end of my life."

When the crowd of people gathered in the foundry heard and saw what Doña Teresa had done, they took off their own rings, chains, crosses, earrings, and bracelets and threw them into the mold.

It is said that no bell ever rang with a sweeter sound.

The foundry workers placed the bell on a ship going to the New World. Many weeks passed before it arrived at the mission. It took a whole day to raise it to the bell tower. The first peals that rang were those of the Angelus, its quiet notes signalling the end of day.

At the exact moment when the bell rang for the first time, Doña Teresa closed her eyes and murmured with her last breath, "Ah, what is that lovely sound? It is the mission bell ringing the Angelus. Don Ángel hears."

The Miracle at the Gate

*(Misión de Nuestra Señora
de la Purísima Concepción de Acuña)*

The Mission of Our Lady of the Immaculate Conception of Acuña was founded in 1716 and dedicated to the Blessed Virgin Mary, the Mother of God. The mission was a fort as well as a church. It sheltered the padres and the peaceful Tejas people from the hard-riding Comanches. Those people loved the wild, free life of their ancestors. They were magnificent horsemen. The soldiers sent to protect the missions could never catch them.

Comanche raiders would attack without warning. They carried off women and children, few of whom were ever seen again. One of the padres always manned a lookout post in the church tower while the Tejas people worked in the fields around the mission.

No Comanches had been seen for a long time. The Tejas workers dug in the fields, preparing the earth for planting. One of the padres went up in the tower to keep watch. Seeing no signs of danger, he opened his prayer book.

He turned the pages, reading each prayer with devotion. He neglected to watch the horizon.

The padre suddenly looked up. In the distance, he saw Comanche horsemen galloping toward the mission. If only he had done his duty! He would have seen the raiders sooner had he not been reading his prayer book. There was only a little time for the people in the fields to run to safety behind the mission walls. The Comanches would be on them in minutes.

The padre raced down the tower stairs. Frantically, he began ringing the mission bell. The other padres came running. The sudden danger presented them with a terrible choice. If they shut the mission gate, the people inside would be safe. But those in the fields would be at the mercy of the Comanches. If they did not shut the gate at once, the Comanches would ride into the mission. Everyone would be at peril.

No one knew what to do. The padres lifted their arms toward heaven, begging for a sign. Then a miracle happened.

A statue of the Virgin Mary stood in a niche above the gate, looking out across the fields. Suddenly the statue began to move. She turned around on her pedestal until she was facing inward, toward the protecting walls.

"The Holy Mother is giving us a sign. She tells us to keep the gate open until all are safe within," the padres cried. They held the gate open as the Tejas people came rushing in from the fields.

The Comanches pursued them up to the gate. It was too late to shut it. The padres and their flock kneeled to pray. Only heaven could protect them now.

But the Comanches did not enter. They rode back and forth before the open gate. Yet they could not pass through. At last they gave up and rode away. The padres watched the raiders vanish over the horizon. Then, singing praises to the Holy Mother, who had saved their lives, they led the way back to the fields.

The Christmas Vine
(Misión de San Antonio de Valero)

The Mission of San Antonio de Valero celebrated its first Christmas in 1718. The padres wanted this Christmas to be special.

One of the padres was a skilled wood-carver. He created a beautiful Nativity scene. People came from miles around to see the Holy Family. They brought gifts for the baby Jesus—shiny stones, bright feathers, a painted pot, strips of red and blue cloth. They were not expensive gifts, but they were beautiful in the eyes of those who brought them. That is what really matters, the padres said. Simple gifts, given with love, are the most precious of all.

Padre Antonio Margil happened to visit the mission at this time. He saw a little boy sitting beside the church door. The boy's head rested on his knees. He would not look up when the padre spoke to him.

Padre Margil sat down beside the boy. "What is wrong, my child?" the priest asked.

The little boy, whose name was Shavano, answered, "Everyone is bringing gifts for the Christ Child. I want to bring a gift, too, but I don't know what it can be. Everything I find seems so ordinary."

Padre Margil replied, "The most precious gifts are the ones that cannot be seen with our eyes. Bring the Christ Child the gift of your heart. There is no greater gift than that."

"I know, Padre," Shavano said, "but I want to bring something I can place before the manger."

"I will help you find it. Bring me an olla, a clay jar. We will search together."

Padre Margil and his friend Shavano went for a walk beyond the mission walls. Along the acequia, the ditch that brings water to the fields, they found a small vine. Its green leaves grew in clusters of three. It bore small green berries.

"This pretty vine will make a fine gift for the Christ Child," Padre Margil said.

"It isn't very beautiful," Shavano replied as he helped the padre dig it up and plant it in the jar. He could not help feeling disappointed.

"Have faith. The Christ Child will make this vine beautiful. You will see," Padre Margil replied.

He and Shavano carried the jar back to the mission church. Shavano helped Padre Margil attach the vine to the front of the manger.

"It still does not look very beautiful," Shavano said.

"It is not Christmas yet," Padre Margil answered.

Shavano came early to church the next morning. As the winter sunlight pierced the shadows, a miracle occurred. The pale, thin vine began to grow until it enfolded the whole manger. Its leaves darkened to a glossy green. The pale berries swelled, turning a vibrant scarlet.

"Oh, Padre! You were right! Our vine is the most beautiful gift of all!" Shavano told Padre Margil. He took the padre by the hand and led him to the manger to show him the miracle he had witnessed.

"We can learn a lesson from the vine," Padre Margil told the people that morning in church. "God's love made a simple vine beautiful. So does God's love for us, and our love for him, make us beautiful. May we all grow together as beautiful vines in God's heavenly garden."

Many years have passed since Padre Margil spoke those words. The Mission of San Antonio de Valero has become the great city of San Antonio. The church is known today as the Alamo. But the little vine like the one Shavano and Padre Margil brought as a gift to the Christ Child still grows wild in parks and fields and along the banks of streams. Its glossy green leaves and scarlet berries continue to decorate churches and Nativity scenes at Christmastime.

It is known as the "Margil Vine."

The Padre's Gift
(Misión de San Antonio de Valero)

The people of San Antonio are known for showing kindness to strangers. Parents have long told their children, "Be courteous to everyone you meet, especially strangers. *¿Quién sabe?* Who knows? Perhaps one day you might be lucky enough to meet the padre."

After the wars with Mexico ended, thousands of yanquis swarmed into Texas. Some of these people were little better than thieves. They would go to the courthouse and file a claim on rich, fertile land that a Tejano family had lived on for generations. When the Tejanos protested, the judge would say to them, "If this land is yours, show us a document to prove it."

Often the only documents they had were old Spanish deeds, land grants from the king of Spain, written in fading ink on crumbling parchment. No one had looked at these documents for a hundred years. In many cases they could no longer be found. No one knew if they still existed.

"In that case, you have no claim to the land at all," said the judge. He would give the land and everything on it to the gringo. The Tejano family would have to leave their home.

One of these yanquis tried to steal a ranch that belonged to the Castro family. The judge gave Señor Castro ten days to produce the original deed. Señor Castro protested that this was unfair. Everyone in San Antonio knew that his family had lived on that land since the days of the missions. He did not know where the deed was. He had never seen it. How could the judge let a stranger take his home?

"The law is the law," the judge said. "You have ten days."

Señor Castro rode home, so overwhelmed by troubles that he failed to notice a person who suddenly appeared beside him.

"Señor Castro?"

Señor Castro looked down. He saw an old, old man walking beside his horse, dressed in the hooded brown robe and sandals that the padres wear. The man's face was leathery brown, broken into fine lines like the cracks in a roof tile. He spoke with the lisping accent of Old Spain.

"I believe I have something that belongs to you." He reached into the pouch that hung from the rope around his waist and took out an envelope made of oiled silk. The red wax seal bore the lions and castles of Old Spain. "Don't break the seal until you get home. Guard what you find inside carefully. Keep it in a safe place and make sure that one person in each generation of your family knows where to find it."

Señor Castro put the envelope in his saddlebag. He turned to thank the stranger, but he had vanished without a trace. Not even the footprints of his sandals remained in the dust of the road.

Señor Castro rode home as fast as his horse could gallop. With his family gathered around, he broke the wax seal on the envelope. He found several sheets of old parchment inside. It was the missing deed to his land.

Not only was it the missing deed, but the writing on it was so clear and so perfectly written that not one single Yanqui scoundrel could challenge it. Several tried. Not one succeeded.

"It was the padre," Señor Castro told his children and grandchildren. "Perhaps one day you will be lucky enough to meet him, too."

There is another story about the mysterious padre. Once the two Fernandez brothers were sent out to water the family's cattle. Francisco and his younger brother, Pedro, herded the cows down to the river. It was a hot, dusty day in July. The boys turned their horses loose and went for a swim in the cool water.

Without warning, a band of Comanches swept down from the hills and drove off the animals. Francisco and Pedro hid in the reeds. The Comanches never found them. Now the boys faced great shame. They had to go home and tell their father that all the family's cattle—all their wealth—was gone.

Francisco and Pedro set out on foot. Along the way they met a padre from one of the missions. At least, he was dressed like a padre. They had never seen him before.

The padre greeted the boys, "*¡Buenos días!*"

"*¡Buenos días, Padre!*" Pedro and Francisco answered.

"I've heard you've had bad luck. It is a shame to lose so many cattle and two fine horses."

Pedro and Francisco wondered how the padre knew about their misfortune. No one else had been with them, and they had told nobody else about it.

"It is hard luck, no doubt," said Francisco. "But it could have been worse. God protected us. The Comanches did not carry us off, as they have done with so many others."

"We have a lot to be thankful for," Pedro agreed. "I only hope that God will continue to protect us. Our father is going to be very angry when we tell him what happened."

The padre smiled. "I don't think he is going to be angry at all." He handed each boy a large leather sack. "Would you do a favor for me? As you walk home, would you keep your eyes open for smooth, flat stones? If you see one, put it in the sack."

"Certainly, Padre," Francisco and Pedro promised. They wondered what use the padre might have for ordinary stones.

The boys continued down the road. It seemed to be full of smooth, flat stones. Pedro and Francisco filled their sacks in no time at all. They walked along, lugging the heavy stones on their backs.

"Why are we carrying these stones?" Pedro asked his brother.

"The padre asked us to. I don't know why he needs them," Francisco answered.

"Do we have to gather so many? Let's throw them away. We'll tell the padre we couldn't find any."

"That would be lying," said Francisco. "Empty your sack, if you wish. I'll keep the stones I have. I'm sure there will be enough for the padre."

Pedro emptied his sack by the side of the road. He continued on with his brother. Home was still several miles away. Francisco's sack of stones grew heavier and heavier. Pedro could see his brother growing tired. He tried to think of some way to help him.

"Francisco," he said, "why don't I carry half those stones? If we share the load, your burden will not be so heavy. I will also be able to say that I found stones and carried them home."

"I knew I could count on you," Francisco said. He poured half the stones into Pedro's sack. The walk home became easier now that both brothers shared the load.

Their parents welcomed them home. "I never thought I would see you boys again," their father said. "Comanche raiders struck all along the river. I feared you had been killed or carried off."

"They stole our cattle and horses," Francisco said.

"But they didn't take our boys. This is what counts," their parents answered.

"What do you have in those sacks?" their sister asked.

Francisco and Pedro emptied their sacks on the patio. Out poured Spanish doubloons, a type of coin that had not been seen for a hundred years.

"¡*Ay!* Why was I so lazy!" Pedro cried. "We would have had twice as many coins if I had filled my sack, too!"

Francisco laughed. "Don't be angry with yourself. We shouldn't be greedy. The padre has given us a generous gift, more than enough to replace our cattle and horses."

"I know," Pedro said, "but if I ever meet the padre again, I am going to do exactly what he says!"

That is what parents in San Antonio tell their children to this day. Always be polite and kind to strangers, especially if they wear brown robes and walk with sandals on their feet.

Who knows, it may be the padre bringing a special gift just for you.

Texas Missions Time Line

1682   Corpus Christi de la Isleta, the first permanent Spanish mission in Texas, is established near El Paso.

1690   San Francisco de los Tejas, the first East Texas mission, is established near Nacogdoches.

1718   The Mission of San Antonio de Valero, now called the Alamo, is founded in San Antonio.

1720   The Mission of San José y San Miguel de Aguayo is founded nearby.

1731   The missions of Our Lady of the Immaculate Conception of Acuña, San Francisco de la Espada, and San Juan Capistrano are established in San Antonio. Fifty-five colonists from the Canary Islands establish a settlement, San Fernando de Béxar.

1758   The Mission of Santa Cruz de San Sabá, near Menard, is destroyed by Comanches.

1793   San Antonio de Valero is secularized. Friars leave. Church property and land are distributed among the settlers.

1803   San Antonio de Valero mission becomes a fort.

1821   Mexico wins independence from Spain.

1836   Texas Republic declares independence from Mexico.

1845   Texas becomes the twenty-eighth state.

Author's Note

I first heard stories about the Texas missions in the spring of 2000 when I visited Sherman, Texas. Belinda Sakowski, the children's librarian at the Sherman Public Library, introduced me to the resources in her collection. There are many variations of the legends about the Spanish missions. In some of the stories, the lady in the blue cloak visits the Jumano people; she has also been seen as far west as New Mexico. In others, she reveals herself to the Tejas people. I decided to base my retellings specifically on Adina de Zavala's *History and Legends of the Alamo and Other Missions in and around San Antonio* (Houston: Arte Público Press, 1996), which, to me, is the most complete and interesting source of the tales. As with all legends, accounts vary widely—years are different, names change. But the spirit of the legends—mysterious and magical— is a result of the remarkable merging of conflicting cultures that took place in this area.

Toucan Valley Publications of Milpitas, California, publishes a series of Texas Mission Fact Cards by Carol Baldridge. These are an excellent introduction to the history, legends, art, and culture of the mission period.